Daniel C Reynolds, Walter Francis Brown

A Romance in Smoke

Daniel C Reynolds, Walter Francis Brown

A Romance in Smoke

ISBN/EAN: 9783337348694

Printed in Europe, USA, Canada, Australia, Japan

Cover: Foto ©Andreas Hilbeck / pixelio.de

More available books at **www.hansebooks.com**

A ROMANCE OF SMOKE

BY DANIEL G. REYNOLDS

WITH ILLUSTRATIONS BY WALTER F. BROWN.

PROVIDENCE
1876.

A Romance in Smoke.

Introduction.

Give the student his meerschaum, the artist his clay;
Let the fisherman doze with his pipe on the bay;
We can smile at the cynic, his ignorance scorn,
And pity the stoic so cold and forlorn:
But that amiable lady disturbs us indeed
Who turns up her nose at the innocent weed;
While the baby is taking a comfortable nap
In the safest of cradles, his dear mother's lap:
While the incense is swinging, O, perfume supreme
From the vale of Havana, the father may dream,
For his bowl of tobacco hath power to invoke
Old memories that lurk in the cloudland of smoke.

Walter F. Brown

Of course, I was young on the day of my birth,
And quite unaccustomed to things here on earth;
But a late conversation with one who was there,
(Now a very old lady of Clavering Square,)
Allows me to say—yes, I own it with shame—
That I acted the pugilist soon as I came,
And made a most strenuous effort to spar,
By clinching both fists at my poor dear mamma;
Such wonderful stories about me are told,
How well I was read at but twenty hours old;
And, unknown in society circles at all,
I opened the season by giving a *bawl*.

There were wretched long hours of colic and pain,
And a host of discomforts encountered in vain;
I was tumbled and tickled, tossed wildly and crushed,
In the arms of fat dowagers frightened and hushed;
I was muffled in laces, worked linen and flannel,
And held in the lap like an overfed spaniel;
I was aired in the gardens by pretty Janet,
Who talked with policemen while I was upset;
Still I throve on misfortune, grew lusty and bold,
And at the right time I was just a year old.

Let me pass over years interesting to none,
Save a nurse or a mother, a midwife or crone,
To those dear little trowsers so wondrously blue,
With *such* rows of gilt buttons all shining and new :
I would call back my feelings of glory and pleasure
Ere my legs fell a prey to the tailor's long measure ;
Let me cling to that time with a shadowless brow,
For I growl at the fellow who measures me now.

There's a quaint little cottage, now empty and cold,
Where a worthy old lady once tended her fold:
What a marvelous treasure of wisdom she taught,
And who can forget the sound thrashings we caught:
She taught us our letters, to sew, and to sing,
Good manners, and many a wonderful thing;
I love to recall her, so many years dead,
When a button flies off and I hunt after thread.

Once a pamphlet appeared, " In the village of Kew,
On a hill-slope commanding a beautiful view,
Where the climate is perfect, the driveways are fine,
With ponds near for bathing and sports with the line :
Here the Reverend Hannibal Lee in the fall
Will open his English and Classical Hall ;
The outfit—a tooth brush, two napkins and ring,
Six shirts and four towels, and that sort of thing :
The object—to furnish young men with the knowledge
Of what is essential to *hang round a college*."

I was packed off to Kew like a prince of a fellow,
With a box full of sweets and a portmanteau yellow,
And Uncle Tom gave me a ten dollar note
To bring down the swelling that rose in my throat.
Ah, those first dreary nights which I spent at the Hall,
When I sobbed in my sleep, I remember them all;
And the Reverend Hannibal Lee—never mind,
He will get his deserts with the rest of mankind,—
I remember *him* culling his classical lore,
And kissing the chamber-maid back of a door.

8

I fell deep in love with a maiden at Kew,
Her hair was so golden, her eyes were so blue:
She was clerk in a bakery close by the Hall,
And her pies were so flakey, her feet were so small:
I made her fine presents, she gave me a cake
With frosting upon it that made my heart ache.
One day in the bake-shop quite lonely I found her,
No one being present my arm stole around her;
Did she lean on my breast, or return my caressing?
No! she rose like a queen and gave me a dressing.
Even now, when I gaze on a cake or a pie,
I feel my ears tingle as if she were nigh.

I next entered college, *conditions* but two,
And my room, number ten, will describe it to you :
Just a snug little chamber in one of the ells,
Where a visitor noticed hospitable smells
Of Perique and Virginia leaf in the air ;
Containing a moth-eaten sofa and chair,
Old pipes by the dozen of china and clay,
A dusty old book-case tucked out of the way,
A coal-hod and shovel, two brooms and a pail,
A pair of worn boxing-gloves hung on a nail,
A cracked chandelier hanging down overhead,
And a very untidy concern called a bed :
All these might be found in my sumptuous den
When I was the freshest and gayest of men.

O that Sophomore hat! can I ever forget it?
(Or how much it cost me one evening to wet it).
When 'twas purchased the hatter looked slyly and said,
" The best looking hat, sir, you've had on your head ; "
Yet I stole down the alleys, and through the dark places,
Like a sinner pursued by immaculate faces ;
But the Freshmen espied it, a whoop and a cry,
And my tile like an eagle took flight to the sky :
Then some Sophomores gave them a glorious dressing,
Returning the hat with a Sophomore's blessing.

I remember when Mac pulled a stroke in the race,
And Dave was sent home to his folks in disgrace,
When I quarreled with Joe for a pretty Miss Dyer,
And bet him a bottle of wine for a flyer
That blue was her color, and teased her to don it
Next Sunday for me on her dear little bonnet:
When Commencement arrived, I had practised a week
On my "Pass at Thermopylæ" essay in Greek.
The old church was packed, how I trembled with fear
At the gaily decked crowds that assembled to hear.
'Tis over, the campus is bleak and forlorn,
The elm trees are sighing, alas they have gone.

Sweet memories of college, how softly they steal
On our hearts in the autumn of life, when we feel
That the frosts of October are near us at last,
And June and her roses have fled with the past :
I can fancy the chapel, the Doctor is there,
His noble white head bended lowly for prayer ;
I can hear the bell tinkle, the service is done,
And the aisles are deserted ; I linger alone.
Alone ? Aye, forever, and listen in vain
For footsteps that ne'er will re-echo again.

My Governor was proud of that Essay in Greek,
And Mother, God bless her, she hardly could speak.
This wonderful genius must travel they said
To strengthen his body and quiet his head ;
Better put him at work old Uncle Tom muttered,
Let the boy earn his bread and find how its buttered ;
There's a banker, a friend in New York, wants a clerk,
He will give our young rascal a touch of hard work.
But my *poor wasted form* on my parents prevailed,
And off on the Java for Europe I sailed.
As I lay in my berth, while the steamer was crossing
The fog banks of Newfoundland, pitching and tossing,
And felt for the basin, methought what a pity
I scornfully fled from that bank in the city :
In those miserable hours of porridge and tea
How I raved at the poets who rave of the sea.

When the crisis was over, a free man again,
How gladly I fled from the tea to champagne;
Yet so terribly altered and shockingly thinner,
Mamma would have wept had she seen me at dinner.
On that memorable day when at last I was able
To gaze with a feverish joy at the table,
(What trivial accidents govern our fate,)
I was timidly trying to balance a plate
Of mulligatawny, the ship gave a swoop,
And into her lap went the hot plate of soup.
O! the ocean's a swell, sweet Madeline Hayes,
And who of us fancies his nautical ways:
But I love to recall that evening in June
When you granted me pardon under the moon.

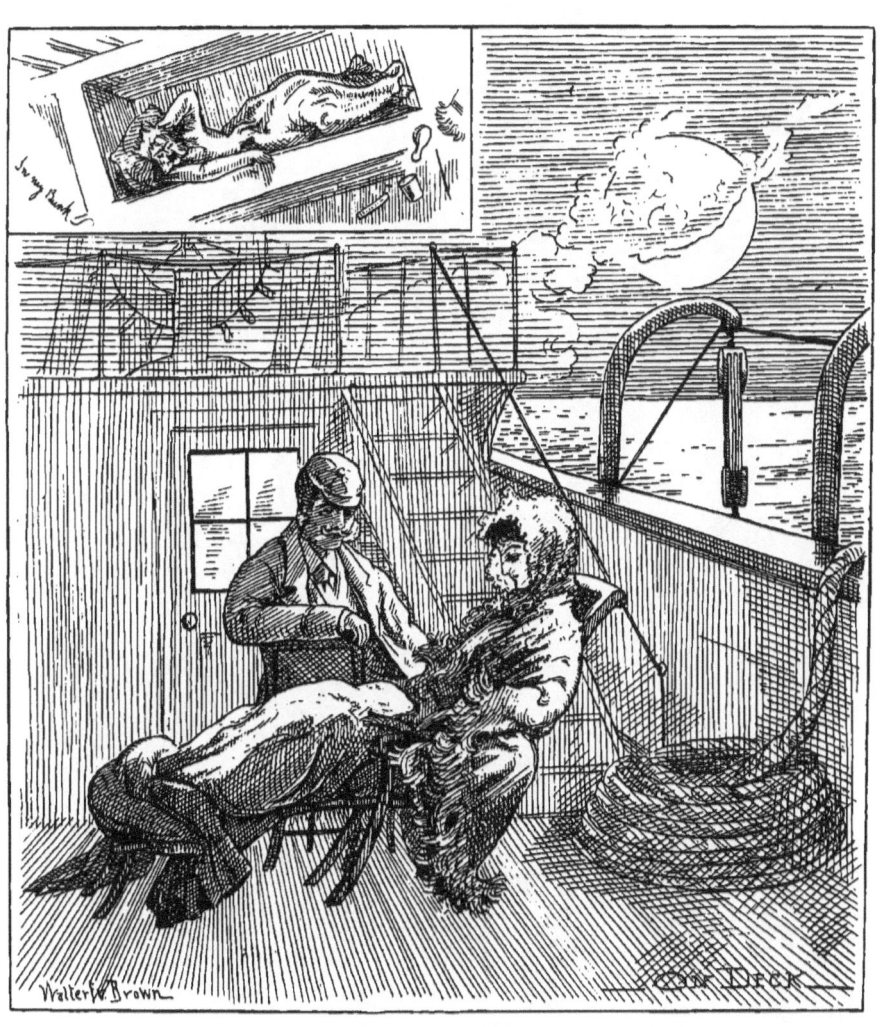

They loitered in London, in paradise I,
With the beautiful face of dear Madeline by;
We visited palaces, galleries and towers,
And lavished on shopping a great many hours,
'Till weary Aunt Bullion declared she must go
To Geneva, away from the Regent St. show,
But would stop at "Paree," just to give her a chance
Of making some purchases travelling through France:
So to Paris we hied. In my fancy I steal,
In the smoke-clouds, a glimpse of the Jardin Mabile.
What a sinner I was, while fair Madeline slept
On her innocent pillow, late vigils I kept
At some sumptuous café; but let it all pass,
My sins were absolved every morning at mass.

Fair Madeline's father and mother were dead,
She was travelling abroad with Aunt Bullion she said ;
For the hot summer months they would stay in Geneva,
'Till Rome might be free of malarious fever ;
Then a glimpse of the ruins, a kiss for the toe
Of the Pope, when to quarters in Paris they'd go :
I told her *my* plans as she sat there beside me,
Poor fellow with only a "Murray" to guide me,
When her aunt, darling woman, near by in a chair,
Half smothered in blankets, on deck for the air,
Suggested she needed a useful young man
To look out for luggage and carry her fan.
O! foolish Aunt Bullion, sweet Madeline Hayes,
How time-like a prodigal squandered his days ;
That night, in a dream, on a huge pile of rope,
A certain young fellow sat fanning the Pope.

But a truce to my bliss, 'twas a letter from home,
A kind, tender letter from old Uncle Tom :
" Your father is ruined, you must not remain
But take the next ship sailing homeward again ;
I would keep you in funds my dear nephew with joy,
But a father in trouble has need of his boy."
Then my beautiful castles all crumbled away,
Rome, Paris, Geneva, alas! where were they ?
When with tremulous voices our farewells were said,
I noticed Miss Madeline's eyelids were red,
But I made no allusion, for that were too bold,
When her Auntie declared she had caught a bad cold.

The tides of misfortune came rolling in fast,
My father's vast wealth was a thing of the past ;
Life's nonsense was over, its work had begun,
And now I must give up devotion to fun,
Pull off yellow kids, neglect my moustache,
Have a higher ambition than making a dash.
Poor father, his black glossy hair had turned white,
He was only a wreck and a pitiful sight ;
The sheriff had gobbled our family estate,
The horses and carriages, jewels and plate,
So we took a neat cottage, quite modest and small,
And Uncle Tom got me a clerkship that fall,
Where the hours were extended, the salary low,
In the great banking house of B. Bullion & Co.

For a year or two life was a drudge and a bore,
But a rift in the clouds showed the sunshine once more :
My salary was doubled, when Bullion & Co.
Decided that into the street I should go,
And attend all the buying and selling of shares,
As well keeping track of the bulls and the bears :
A few lucky hits, when the bears were all short,
And a twist of my own, where the bulls were all caught,
Gave me prestige and fame, so what could I fear,
I was sailing ahead on three thousand a year.

One morning old Bullion tossed over a letter—
" Look here, they've arrived, and I think you had better
Go down on the tug and get my folks through
The Custom House safely, I've all I can do."
The message ran thus—"The French steamer Greece
Is rounding the Hook with your Madame and niece."
O! what to my wonder, surprise and delight
Was the beautiful vision that burst on my sight ;
When I boarded the steamer, Aunt Bullion was there
And my own little Madeline looking so fair.
But alas ! by her side stood a young foreign swell
Quite lost in an ulster, my heart how it fell
When she called him Ricardo.   I fled with a sigh.
Nor waited to bid them a civil good-bye.

This must be her lover, a sprig of a lord,
Some bit of nobility picked up abroad,
And I am discarded, remembered no more,—
She is only a trifler I savagely swore.
Thus I raved like a madman for nearly a week,
Not eating, nor sleeping, I hardly could speak ;
But my anger subsiding, I ventured to call
One evening on Madeline, telling her all,
How I loved her so fondly, so long and so true,
When she slyly looked up, saying, "and I love *you*.
The foreign young man who has caused you this pain
Is a cook that Aunt Bullion imported from Spain."

Aunt Bullion got mad when I asked for her neice,—
"Well take the poor child, only leave me in peace;
She is young, very young, why she only can make
The heaviest of bread and the dryest of cake;
You still want my darling? then there's my consent,"
And off to the parlor betrothed we went,
Where we sat in the twilight together quite late
With a long hour of parting below at the gate.
Next evening I called on my angel and brought her
A diamond ring of the very first water,
And often, so often my fond gaze would linger
O'er that wee little ring on a wee little finger.

The wedding day came, 'twas a lovely affair,
So a lady informed me who chanced to be there;
The presents were royal, the supper was fine,
The music entrancing, the toilets divine.
But I only remember my sweet little bride
In a halo of lace as she stood by my side,
And they say that I did a most blundering thing
When the clergyman told me to put on the ring;
But what do I care, since I'm married at last,
Sure the wedding and blunder are things of the past:
Now the latest achievement that gives me such joy
Is a jolly ten pounder, a live kicking boy.

———

Hark! baby's awake, I can tell by the shout,
The romance is over, my pipe has gone out.

Walter Fr. Brown —